NORTHSIDE   Y0-EJA-309
804 131st AVE. NE
BLAINE, MN 55434

BASKETBALL LEGENDS

Kareem Abdul-Jabbar

Charles Barkley

Larry Bird

Wilt Chamberlain

Clyde Drexler

Julius Erving

Patrick Ewing

Anfernee Hardaway

Grant Hill

Magic Johnson

Michael Jordan

Jason Kidd

Reggie Miller

Hakeem Olajuwon

Shaquille O'Neal

Scottie Pippen

David Robinson

Dennis Rodman

CHELSEA HOUSE PUBLISHERS

Basketball Legends

REGGIE MILLER

Barry Wilner

Introduction by
Chuck Daly

CHELSEA HOUSE PUBLISHERS
Philadelphia

Produced by Daniel Bial and Associates
New York, New York

Picture research by Alan Gottlieb
Cover illustration by Bradford Brown

Copyright © 1998 by Chelsea House Publishers, a division of Main Line Book Co. All rights reserved. Printed and bound in the United States of America.

First Printing

1 3 5 7 9 8 6 4 2

Library of Congress Cataloging-in-Publication Data

Wilner, Barry.
    Reggie Miller / Barry Wilner ; introduction by Chuck Daly.
      p. cm. -- (Basketball legends)
    Includes bibiliographical references and index.
    Summary: A look at the personal life and basketball career of the high-scoring Indiana Pacer, known almost as much for his verbal antics as for his shooting prowess.
    ISBN 0-7910-4384-3
    1. Miller, Reggie, 1965- --Juvenile literature. 2. Basketball players--United States--Biography--Juvenile literature.
[1. Miller, Reggie, 1965- 2. Basketball players. 3. Afro-Americans--Biography.] I. Title. II. Series.
GV884.M556W55   1997
796.323'092--dc21
[B]   97-14224
                                                         CIP
                                                          AC

CONTENTS

BECOMING A
BASKETBALL LEGEND   6

CHAPTER 1
REGGIE'S GREATEST   9

CHAPTER 2
REGGIE'S CHILDHOOD   17

CHAPTER 3
ALL-AMERICAN   25

CHAPTER 4
ROOKIE   33

CHAPTER 5
ALL-STAR   43

CHAPTER 6
DREAM TEAMER   55

STATISTICS   61
CHRONOLOGY   62
FURTHER READING   63
INDEX   64

BECOMING A BASKETBALL LEGEND

Chuck Daly

What does it take to be a basketball superstar? Two of the three things it takes are easy to spot. Any great athlete must have excellent skills and tremendous dedication. The third quality needed is much harder to define, or even put in words. Others call it leadership or desire to win, but I'm not sure that explains it fully. This third quality relates to the athlete's thinking process, a certain mentality and work ethic. One can coach athletic skills, and while few superstars need outside influence to help keep them dedicated, it is possible for a coach to offer some well-timed words in order to keep that athlete fully motivated. But a coach can do no more than appeal to a player's will to win; how much that player is then capable of ensuring victory is up to his own internal workings.

In recent times, we have been fortunate to have seen some of the best to play the game. Larry Bird, Magic Johnson, and Michael Jordan had all three components of superstardom in full measure. They brought their teams to numerous championships, and made the players around them better. (They also made their coaches look smart.)

I myself coached a player who belongs in that class, Isiah Thomas, who helped lead the Detroit Pistons to consecutive NBA crowns. Isiah is not tall—he's just over six feet—but he could do whatever he wanted with the ball. And what he wanted to do most was lead and win.

All the players I mentioned above and those whom this series will chronicle are tremendously gifted athletes, but for the most part, you can't play professional basketball at all unless you have excellent skills. And few players get to stay on their team unless they are willing to dedicate themselves to improving their talents even more, learning about their opponents, and finding a way to join with their teammates and win.

It's that third element that separates the good player from the superstar, the memorable players from the legends of the game. Superstars know when to take over the game. If the situation calls for a defensive stop, the superstars stand up and do it. If the situation calls for a key pass, they make it. And if the situation calls for a big shot, they want the ball. They don't want the ball simply because of their own glory or ego. Instead they know—and their teammates know—that they are the ones who can deliver, regardless of the pressure.

The words "legend" and "superstar" are often tossed around without real meaning. Taking a hard look at some of those who truly can be classified as "legends" can provide insight into the things that brought them to that level. All of them developed their legacy over numerous seasons of play, even if certain games will always stand out in the memories of those who saw them. Those games typically featured amazing feats of all-around play. No matter how great the fans thought the superstars were, these players were capable of surprising the fans, their opponents, and occasionally even themselves. The desire to win took over, and with their dedication and athletic skills already in place, they were capable of the most astonishing achievements.

CHUCK DALY, most recently the head coach of the New Jersey Nets, guided the Detroit Pistons to two straight NBA championships, in 1989 and 1990. He earned a gold medal as coach of the 1992 U.S. Olympic basketball team—the so-called "Dream Team"—and was inducted into the Pro Basketball Hall of Fame in 1994.

1
REGGIE'S GREATEST

Whenever the New York Knicks and Indiana Pacers faced each other in the playoffs, sparks seemed bound to fly. They rarely flew so high, though, than in the fifth game of the 1994 Eastern Conference finals. On June 1, the New York Knicks were leading the series three games to one and looking to salt away the win on their home turf, Madison Square Garden. They came into the fourth quarter with a 12-point lead, but suddenly they ran into a buzzsaw named Reggie Miller.

Miller, Indiana's shooting guard, had not had a particularly good game so far. He had tried 16 shots in the first three quarters and made only six for a total of 14 points. But the Knicks knew they could not rest easy. Miller had a reputation as a streak shooter—someone who could get hot

John Starks watches in dismay as Reggie Miller sinks yet another three-pointer. Miller scored 39 points to help the Pacers defeat the Knicks at Madison Square Garden in the fifth game of the 1994 playoffs between these two teams.

Reggie took on not only the physical play of the Knicks . . .

at any time. If he got hot, he could change the course of a game in a hurry.

Miller also had a reputation as someone who liked to shoot off his mouth and could get under the skin of opposing players and fans. Before this game was over, he would prove both reputations were well earned.

Miller's first shot of the period was a three-point jump shot on a fast break. Swish.

"The Knicks who were back didn't come out and I had plenty of room to just pull up and shoot," Miller says. "Whenever I see that, I'll take it."

Reggie scored again 47 seconds later, knocking in another three-pointer, this time with Hubert Davis guarding him. Davis was also a sharpshooter, but he was not known for his defense as Reggie is. "I knew I could run circles around Hubert," Miller says. "My theory on shots when I'm all alone is that I should make 70 percent of them. I don't think other players set standards that high and that's a mistake."

Just over a minute later, Miller hit a two-pointer over Greg Anthony, who gives away five inches to the Pacers' shooting guard.

Still, nobody was getting really excited. The favored Knicks still had the lead and Miller was known to go through streaks. "I definitely can go through those things when I get real hot and hit everything I try," he says. "Then I can turn cold and miss, too. But I had a real feel for the way things were going."

Miller used a set of picks—when a teammate puts his body in the way of the defender to free the shooter—to get his fourth basket, another two-pointer. He looked like a man trying to avoid stepping into puddles during a rainstorm as he ran around those picks to get open.

On that shot, Miller was so open he could have dribbled back two steps and let go a three. He didn't even think about it. "I never want to be conscious of the line. I never get ticked off, like some guys do, if my foot is on the line and I get a two instead of a three," he says. "It's too difficult just to get open. My eyes are looking ahead of me, to the point where I'm going to get the pass and take my shot, so they can't be looking down at the floor."

With the scored tied at 72 and Indiana having possession, the fans were getting nervous. Coach Pat Riley told his Knicks to

. . . He also welcomed the taunting of director Spike Lee, who tried to razz Miller from his courtside seat.

keep the ball out of Miller's hands at any cost, but Reggie worked his way out past the top of the key and took a pass from a teammate. He wasn't standing in New Jersey when he put the shot up. It only seemed Miller was that far from the hoop. Despite standing five feet behind the three-point line, he quickly released the ball and watched it go through the net.

"He was in the Twilight Zone," said Derek Harper, one of the Knick guards victimized by Miller. "When a guy gets hot like that, it's hard to stop him. . . . He carried the team on his back and his teammates fed off of his heroics."

The television announcers hardly could believe Miller would throw up a shot from "beyond downtown." But this was Reggie Miller, and when he is feeling good, feeling on-target, he's apt to shoot from any distance.

Reggie also is known for how fast he releases his shots. The next three-pointer came on an incredibly quick shot with John Starks all over him.

The year before, Starks and Miller had a famous run-in. Starks, an All Star that year, couldn't handle Miller's offense or his trash-talking. In frustration, the volatile Starks head-butted Miller in the third game of the series. The referees ejected Starks. He left with his team leading 59-57. Miller made two free throws awarded for the flagrant foul, igniting a 19-4 spurt that put the Pacers ahead to stay.

Unlike Hubert Davis, Starks was known for playing a good defense. However, when Reggie hit his sixth basket of the fourth quarter of his greatest game, he said, "John was almost crying."

Reggie, having already abused Starks, Davis, Harper, and Anthony, next took on the entire

New York team. When he tried another long shot from just in front of the Knicks' bench, he kept his right arm extended in the air after letting the ball go, showing utmost confidence that his aim was perfect. A disinterested spectator—and there wasn't a single such person in the entire crowd—might have felt Reggie was showboating.

"I don't do it to taunt anyone," he says with a smile. "I do it because when my father taught me to shoot, he taught me to extend that arm and keep it up there real high."

Miller was making the Knicks and their fans feel real low. By now, his run had the Pacers in control and the crowd in a frustrated lather.

"Playing in the Garden, people just don't understand the odds. My object is to go in there and make 19,000 people boo Patrick Ewing. That's the best," he says. Ewing, the Knicks star center, was trying to rally New York, but was unable to counteract Miller's fireworks.

Reggie had one other target for his attentions. Spike Lee, famed director of such movies as "Do the Right Thing" and "She's Gotta Have It," was an avid Knicks fan and perennial front-row spectator. Lee and Miller conducted a running conversation throughout the period. Reggie often gestured at Lee after making a basket, later claiming it was all in fun.

Spike had a bet with Miller about the series. If the Pacers won, Lee would give Reggie's wife, Marita, a role in his next film. If the Knicks won, Miller would visit boxer Mike Tyson in prison.

Miller's phenomenal shooting and playmaking had not only dispirited the Knicks, it had made Spike Lee an enemy in New York for a few days after Miller Time played the Garden. "They're killing me now, like I threw the ball away six times in a row," Lee said of the reaction around New York to his part in setting off Miller. "Like I'm responsible for a 23-3 run. That's a joke. That's garbage. I did not provoke him. [Reggie] wants to beat the Knicks, not Spike Lee."

But Antonio Davis, a teammate of Miller's, claimed Lee positively helped Miller get going. "Spike definitely said something that set him off," Pacers forward Antonio Davis said. "I'm not sure what it was, but Reggie took us on a ride after that."

At the final horn, the Pacers walked off with a 93-86 victory. During the 12 minutes of the fourth quarter, Miller made five three-pointers, three regular baskets, and four free throws for a total of 25 points. It was arguably the best long-range shooting performance in NBA playoffs history. Almost single-handedly Miller had saved Indiana from elimination and sent the series back to Indianapolis with the Pacers having all the momentum.

After the game, Miller was a bit surprised at his streak. "I felt good, but I can't say I expected things to happen the way they did," Miller says. "I guess you get into a zone or something and the shots drop from everywhere."

"I've never seen anything like it with so much at stake," Pacers coach Larry Brown says. "Here's a guy who had played in the league six years and done pretty well. But most people thought that Reggie was just a guy that shot the ball and shot his mouth off."

Oddly, after his best performance, Miller was more drained than thrilled. "What I do remember is coming back on the bus ride home and having the worst migraine I've ever had before," he said. "If that's what the zone feels like, I don't want a lot of them, because my head felt like it was going to pop open."

Reggie and Spike Lee popped up together on the "Late Show with David Letterman" after the series. Letterman was interviewing Miller when Lee made a surprise walk-on appearance. He was holding a blue Knicks road jersey and wearing a 1994 NBA Finals cap. After an embrace, Lee gave Miller the jersey, which had Starks' number 3 on it—not exactly the perfect gift, but it drew lots of laughs.

Letterman asked Miller what went on between him and Lee during Game 5.

"I wasn't having a very good game and he was kind of ribbing me," Miller said. "After I hit that first three, I kind of looked at him and started talking to him, and after that, it was history. I just told him about a few of his movies that weren't doing so well."

Another bull's-eye for Reggie Miller.

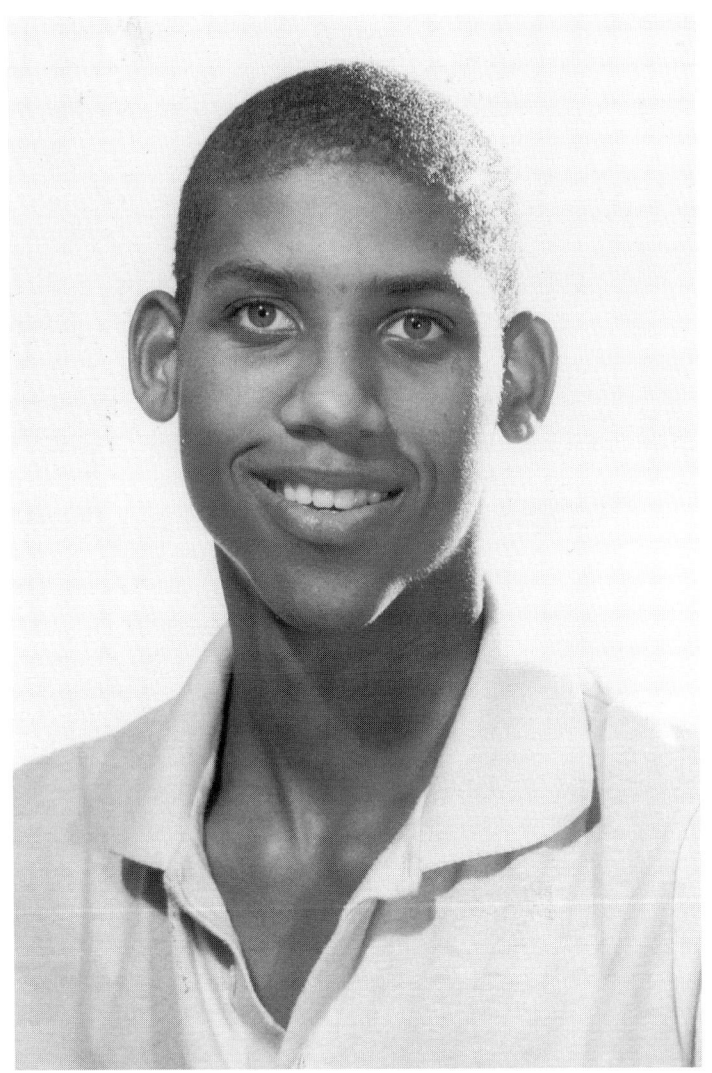

2
REGGIE'S CHILDHOOD

Reggie Miller had to be special just to keep up with his brothers and sisters.

The fourth of five children born to Saul and Carrie Miller, Reggie never got a chance to hog the spotlight while growing up in Riverside, California.

His eldest brother, Saul, Jr., followed in his father's footsteps and became a world-class saxophonist. The next brother, Darrell, was a catcher for the California Angels who then went into front office work. Then came Cheryl, who was an outstanding basketball player in high school and college. Every year she was voted an All-American. Cheryl Miller is considered the greatest women's basketball player ever.

So Reggie—who also has a younger sister, Tammy, who played volleyball and now is a lawyer—had some serious competition in his own home.

As a child, Reggie wore braces on his legs for four years and several doctors thought he might never walk properly.

Reggie's sister Cheryl may have been the greatest female basketball player ever. Here she celebrates with her parents, Saul and Carrie, after leading the U.S team to a gold medal at the 1984 Olympics.

"He had to struggle to survive in the house," Saul said. "Everyone being an athlete and being older, they were somewhat more talented and slightly ahead of him. Reggie always had to work hard."

"Actually, it was the greatest thing that could have happened for me," Reggie said. "I had the best support anyone could want and the best advice and the best family situation.

"I was so scared of my parents that if I did anything wrong, my conscience would kill me. Wow, I'd be guilt-ridden. But I'm glad I had the upbringing I did. You know, in today's society, kids sometimes have no conscience about right and wrong. But my family was almost perfect and I was very lucky."

Reggie's Childhood

When Reggie was born on August 24, 1965, he had some physical problems that worried his parents. His hips weren't properly developed, forcing his ankles to turn inward. For nearly four years, he was forced to wear braces on his legs and several doctors claimed he might never walk properly.

But when Reggie's braces were removed, he was liked an unchained animal, anxious to burn off all the energy stored inside. He'd shoot hoops with the family on the driveway basketball court Saul built to help his children's games, and see nearly every shot get blocked.

"Did you ever wonder where I got that high arc on my shot?" he asks. "I got tired of seeing the ball back in my face as a kid, when one of my brothers or Cheryl would block it. So I had to learn something else."

Growing up, Reggie always had to strive for more just to be on a par with his older siblings. For example, on that driveway court, Reggie quickly found a need for more room. Already in love with long-range bombing, Reggie would move farther and farther back, until his shots were coming from his mother's flower bed.

"I destroyed countless flowers," Reggie remembers, "and it seemed like I was always getting in trouble for it."

Carrie Miller and the rest of the clan realized that Reggie's ability to hit from downtown—or down among the flowers—was a skill to nurture, not discourage. "I could tell he could be a shooter. It always came easy to him," Saul said. "We built that half-court in the backyard and it was 23 feet from the outside. Reggie started to hit from there and, next thing you knew, he was trying from further out. So I added nine feet to the court, and that put him in the flower beds."

"It just became a habit, shooting long," Reggie said. "I would stay out there all day, all night, just shooting by myself and pretending I was playing with the greatest players, like Wilt Chamberlain and Jerry West. I would play games, all by myself, and announce them or have crowd noises and it would drive my mom crazy."

Like several other basketball stars—including Michael Jordan—Reggie's best sport as a teenager was baseball. "Back then, I would have said he'd be a major league baseball player if he made it in any sport," Saul said. "I believe all of us would. The high school coaches couldn't wait to get ahold of Reggie."

Once, when he was 9 years old, Reggie hit a ball so far it broke a window in a house a block away. The tenant of the house came out to scold the boys and refused to believe it was little Reggie—who was playing with two older, bigger friends—who hit the ball.

Baseball, however, did not hold the attraction for Reggie that basketball did. "In basketball, every play has a level of excitement and everyone on the court and in the stands is into it," Miller said. "In baseball, the only time people got excited was if you hit a home run or stole a base. I need the high of basketball."

But the court would also become an unfair proving ground for Reggie. Because Cheryl was nearly 20 months older—and, of course, because she was so much better than her competition—Reggie's achievements paled in comparison.

By the time she was nine, Cheryl was a regular on the family court, knocking down jump shots and no longer being intimidated by her brothers and their buddies.

She was a star even before she became an All-American at Riverside Poly High School. Then she became a legend—on the same day Reggie would make a personal breakthrough.

It was Reggie's first start as a sophomore at Poly, and he lit up the crowd and the scoreboard by scoring 39 points. He raced home to tell Cheryl, whose team had played at roughly the same time.

"They started me and I got 39," Reggie told her with a big smile and a strong sense of pride.

"Reggie, that's great," Cheryl responded.

Then she hit him with her news. "He asked me how many I scored and I said, '105.' He said, 'Come on, no way.' But I repeated it and he knew it was true."

Reggie then picked up a basketball and went to the backyard to practice his shooting.

"It was hard following Cheryl," he admitted. "With brothers, it's two guys competing, so it's no big deal. A sister, being in a male-dominated world—as they say—everybody is going to say something.

"In my situation, I understand that, because Cheryl is the best and there won't ever be anyone better in women's basketball. But she helped my drive tremendously. The pressure helped me raise my game. For every four or five accolades she got, I would just try to get one or two."

Reggie never tried to get 105. He knew that was not challengeable. Only Wilt Chamberlain had ever scored 100 points in an NBA game. Only Furman Selvy had ever scored 100 in an NCAA college game. No man ever scored more than 100 at that level; indeed they are the only two ever to have broken 90. Cheryl's 105 meant

Reggie's brother Darrell was a catcher for the California Angels.

she had scored more points in one game than any big-time male player.

But Reggie knew Cheryl was challengeable. At some point, Reggie figured, he'd be able to take her on the family court, just for fun.

That day came after Cheryl had gone to the University of Southern California, where she would have a Hall of Fame career. One day during her freshman season, she was back in Riverside and she told Reggie, "Let's go have a game."

It didn't last long. Reggie had grown to 6'7". Even though Cheryl stood 6'2", Reggie now towered over "big sister." He blocked her first shot against the backboard, and that was all Cheryl needed to see.

"Let's play H-O-R-S-E instead," she said.

There's never been any jealousy between Reggie and Cheryl. Rather, they are each other's biggest fans.

"She is my closest friend," he said. "In the family, we're all close. But Cheryl and I are the closest, along with my parents."

Still, Reggie knows Cheryl will always cast something of a shadow over him. "Until the day I die, I will always be known as Cheryl Miller's little brother, even if I'm a six-time MVP, all-star and on a championship team."

At USC, Cheryl won two national championships. She also won a gold medal at the 1984 Olympics. But her superb college career didn't lead to any rich professional contracts. Instead, she tried coaching (at USC) and then took up television broadcasting.

"When you look at what I accomplished, it isn't fair," she said. "But, hey, that's life. Now I root for Reggie."

Rooting for Reggie was not disappointing. At Riverside Poly, he averaged 27 points a game and led the team to the California high school championship as a junior. The next year, he upped his scoring to 30 points a game, won another state title, and, like Cheryl, made All-America.

Schools from throughout the United States recruited Reggie. He wanted to stay local. His main choices were USC, where Cheryl already was a megastar, or its crosstown rival, UCLA, the most successful program in college basketball history.

"When I was growing up, UCLA was on TV all the time," he said. "John Wooden was the greatest coach and Pauley Pavilion was the place to play. I had to wear the blue and gold."

3
ALL-AMERICAN

Pauley Pavilion is the temple of college basketball, the home of champions, the place where the most NCAA tournament banners hang and the most memories of success linger.

It has been the sporting home of John Wooden, Lew Alcindor (who later changed his name to Kareem Abdul-Jabbar and became the NBA's all-time leading scorer), Bill Walton, Walt Hazzard, Gail Goodrich, Marques Johnson, and Sidney Wicks. All greats, members of various Halls of Fame.

That had to impress a teen-age basketball star, especially one who grew up nearby. And with his older sister Cheryl establishing herself as the ultimate star of the women's game at crosstown rival Southern California, going to UCLA seemed like a natural decision for Reggie Miller.

UCLA has won more NCAA championships than any other team. Although Reggie never got to play in a Final Four game while with UCLA, he still ranked in the Top 10 in UCLA history in every important scoring category.

In a 1986 game against Arizona State, Reggie is double-teamed by Alex Austin (number 23) and Bobby Thompson (number 21).

"When you walk into Pauley, you feel the ghosts and the dreams," Miller said. "With all the banners, there's a feeling of winning, and I'm proud I could contribute to that."

Walt Hazzard was Reggie's coach at UCLA and knew the gossip Reggie had deal with. "Reggie would hear all these people saying, 'That's Cheryl Miller's brother. He can't even play with her,'" said Hazzard. "That would get Reggie motivated to prove himself, prove he could play the game."

Coach Larry Farmer recruited Reggie, but Hazzard took over as head coach while Miller was a rookie in 1984, and Miller quickly proved himself to Hazzard. "This youngster has the potential to be a superstar," Hazzard told Reggie's parents. "He's going to be a superstar."

On the way to stardom, there were some unhappy incidents at UCLA that helped Reggie gain a reputation as a loudmouth. Once, when he was a sophomore, the Bruins were playing against Brigham Young University. An opponent spat on one of the Bruins, so Miller spat back.

Reggie was also branded a trash-talker, an image that stuck with him right into the NBA.

Cheryl thinks that reputation has always been unfair. "I have to admit, he's very emotional, very excitable, and he wears his emotions on his sleeves," she said. "Everybody thought he was a flamboyant, cocky hot dog. Those were bad tags, given to Reggie for no reason. They just didn't understand how competive Reggie is."

In one big game in New York against St. John University, an injured Miller had a poor outing against forward Willie Glass. Miller scored 18 points, nine below his average at the time, with only two in the first half.

"You have to give credit to Willie Glass for the tremendous job he did on Reggie Miller," said St. John's coach Lou Carnesecca, ignoring that Miller had a tender ankle.

"Willie Glass says he is the best defensive player in the country," countered Hazzard. "Well, today, he played a one-legged man. Reggie Miller was 60 percent of himself."

Although Miller never publicly complained, some media members dubbed him a "crybaby."

That same season, Miller was given a technical foul for throwing the ball at Cal's Kevin Johnson. He also was accused of rubbing his fingers together in the common sign for someone seeking money, aiming the gesture at a referee during a game against the University of Arizona. Miller seemed to be asserting the referee was "on the take," or being paid to make calls for one team and against the other; however, he never was penalized as the ref didn't see the gesture.

Arizona coach Lute Olson accused Reggie of a cheap shot during a brawl at Pauley Pavilion, even though nearly every player involved was out of control.

Could all of this be attributed to enthuasiam, as Cheryl Miller suggests? Even Reggie confessed that he had earned some of his negative reputation.

"I'll admit that I do some things purposely, at times, for effect," he said. "When we need the crowd to react, I'll do some antics out there. On the road, too, I'll play to the crowd sometimes. And I'll admit that sometimes I get carried away. Sometimes you wish you could turn back the hands of the clock and have a chance to do something differently.

"When I step on the court, I become a totally different person," he added. "Some people call me a jerk, a whiner. I might be when I step on the court. But as soon as I go to the lockerroom, I'm cool. When I'm out to dinner, people come up to talk to me and I'm nice."

Unfortunately, not everyone watching Reggie play has understood that the bad Reggie is not the only Reggie. The confusion was at its height when he was at UCLA.

"He's spirited," said Hazzard. "He doesn't like to get pushed around. He's not a wimp. People say he's a thin kid that can just shoot and all you have to do is bust him in the chest and he'll disappear.

"Coaches do that, you know," Hazzard continued. "They send people out there just to push him and jump around and throw him off his game. He's a target, and when you're a target, the eyes of people are on you and other teams draw up schemes to stop you. It's something he's had to learn to deal with."

Hazzard knew not to let Reggie go to far. "The way I deal with it is to take him out when I think he's off-base. I don't think you let someone push you around, but you have to pick the proper time and way to get it done. You have to let them know you're not going to take it."

Reggie's way sometimes involved his mouth or his temper. More often, it centered on long shots flying through the hoop, and lots of points flickering onto the scoreboard.

Only Alcindor had more 30-point games at UCLA. Lew had 27 in his storied career to 16 for Miller. Only Alcindor and Bill Walton had bigger scoring efforts than Miller's career-high 42 against Louisville in 1987, a game of which Louisville assistant coach Wade Houston said, "He taught our guys a lesson, doing everything we teach them not to allow. We tell them never to allow someone to go baseline, and he went baseline all night."

No Bruin ever made more than the 202 free throws Miller canned in 1986. This statistic shows that Reggie was not a one-dimensional player in college. You simply don't get to the free throw line that often if you are bombing away from outside.

"Reggie can do just about everything," said Pooh Richardson, who was the point guard for the Bruins in Miller's senior year. "He might be

After leading UCLA to a 65-62 win over Indiana University in the 1985 NIT championship, Miller was voted the tournament's Most Valuable Player.

the best guy on the drive in college basketball. He knows he can beat his man and get the basket or get to the line."

Miller ranks in the top 10 in UCLA history in every important scoring category. Yet his image was what people seemed to concentrate on more than the substance of his game.

Reggie didn't mind. "I like my bad boy image," he said as a senior. "It's gotten me a lot of places. I was this skinny kid when I started and no one thought I was tough. But I'm a hard-nosed kid who likes to play hard. People don't know about all the dirty stuff underneath the basket, when I get elbows in the ribs and shoves from behind. They only see me throw the elbow back. There are two sides to every coin and everyone only sees heads. My side is tails."

Reggie worked his tail off in pickup games during the summer in the Los Angeles area, games that featured NBA stars Magic Johnson and Byron Scott of the Lakers. Scott even gave Miller tips on how to upgrade his game, particularly his shot release. "A lot of people didn't think he would make it," Scott said. "All they saw was this skinny kid from UCLA who liked to talk. But he had this attitude of, 'I'm gonna show you.' I liked that. I could relate to that."

Miller was unable to help bring another NCAA championship to UCLA, but he helped bring back the tradition of success. The Bruins had four winning seasons when he was on the team, won the NIT in 1984-85—with Miller as MVP of the tournament—and were 25-7, with a Pacific-10 Conference title in his senior year. Overall, UCLA was 78-44 with Miller on the roster, and Reggie made the all-conference team twice, as well as several All-America lists. Three times, he won the team's most valuable player honors. The one season he didn't was 1984, his freshman year, when Reggie was selected the best rookie among the Bruins.

Miller, who majored in communications—a fitting subject for someone who likes to talk so much—wrapped up his collegiate career in 1987.

Hazzard summed up his star player's potential. "His greatest asset is his determination and his competitiveness," Hazzard said. "He's worked very hard to become better, and he loves the challenge."

The challenge would become stronger as a pro.

4
ROOKIE

For years, Reggie Miller was used to being watched by scouts. At practices, in games, at tournaments, they always were there. From high school straight through his four strong seasons at UCLA, they observed, they took notes, they decided just how good a player he was. When the scouts returned to their home office, they brought back reports on Reggie that sometimes glowed with enthusiasm—and sometimes mentioned reservations.

"A pure shooter who isn't afraid to put it up from outside in any situation," one evaluation said. "He'll take the shot to win the game, and if he misses, he'll take it again the next time."

"He's improved every area," wrote another, "but still is best when shooting the ball. Has never seen a shot he didn't like, and can make many of them. Great confidence on offense, and his

As a rookie, Miller showed no fear of more established players. Here, as Boston's Danny Ainge looks on, Miller goes to the hoop against Larry Bird while Robert Parrish waits to try to block his shot.

defense is better than ever. But he's not going to stop many NBA guards. Needs to learn to rebound better for someone his size. Has good attitude, tough, but also talks too much and will get penalized for it in pros."

Other reports called him inconsistent, selfish, and star-struck. One scout believed he was so weak defensively that he'd never be able to hold opponents to fewer points than he scored.

"You can't really worry about what people say," Miller said. "If you get off to a good start, you can always turn it around and make them feel good about you. If I get off to a good start and play consistently during the whole year, then everybody's going to be patting me on the back, saying, 'What a great pick!'"

As Miller approached the 1987 draft, he began studying his geography. There was a good chance he would wind up back East, perhaps in New Jersey with the Nets, in Washington with the Bullets, or in Cleveland with the Cavaliers. All these teams had high picks and could use a pure shooter such as Reggie.

Miller, however, preferred to stay in southern California. Still, he understood how the process worked and that he had no real options but to join the team that selected him. "I knew the chances weren't very good for me to stay home, unless the Clippers wanted me," he said. "The Lakers weren't even picking in the first round, and the Clippers were talking about taking a forward."

That the Los Angeles Clippers, whose history in the draft rivals the worst in any sport, would ignore the local kid was sad. They didn't have a topnotch scorer, and Miller always was lighting it up just a few miles away.

After Miller almost single-handedly destroyed Southern Cal as a senior, Trojan coach Stan Morrison wondered if the executives of the Clippers, who played their home games at the Sports Arena — also Southern Cal's court — were on hand. "Reggie put on a show," he said. "All the Clippers had to do was step out of their offices. He's a great player. He's gone from a one-dimensional player to a three-dimensional one. He can shoot outside, he can put it on the floor and he's outstanding without the ball."

Of course, in retrospect, Reggie would happily tell you he's glad that the Clippers didn't draft him. It would take 10 years before the team would even reach a mediocre level of play.

The San Antonio Spurs had the first choice and even though he wouldn't be eligible to play for them for at least a year, they grabbed Navy's David Robinson, who had just won the title of college player of the year. The Phoenix Suns wanted a power forward and took Armon Gilliam of the University of Nevada, Las Vegas next.

An hour passed, and Reggie still was not taken. Team after team passed by Miller—and only later would learn their mistake. The New Jersey Nets took guard Dennis Hopson of Ohio State; sup-

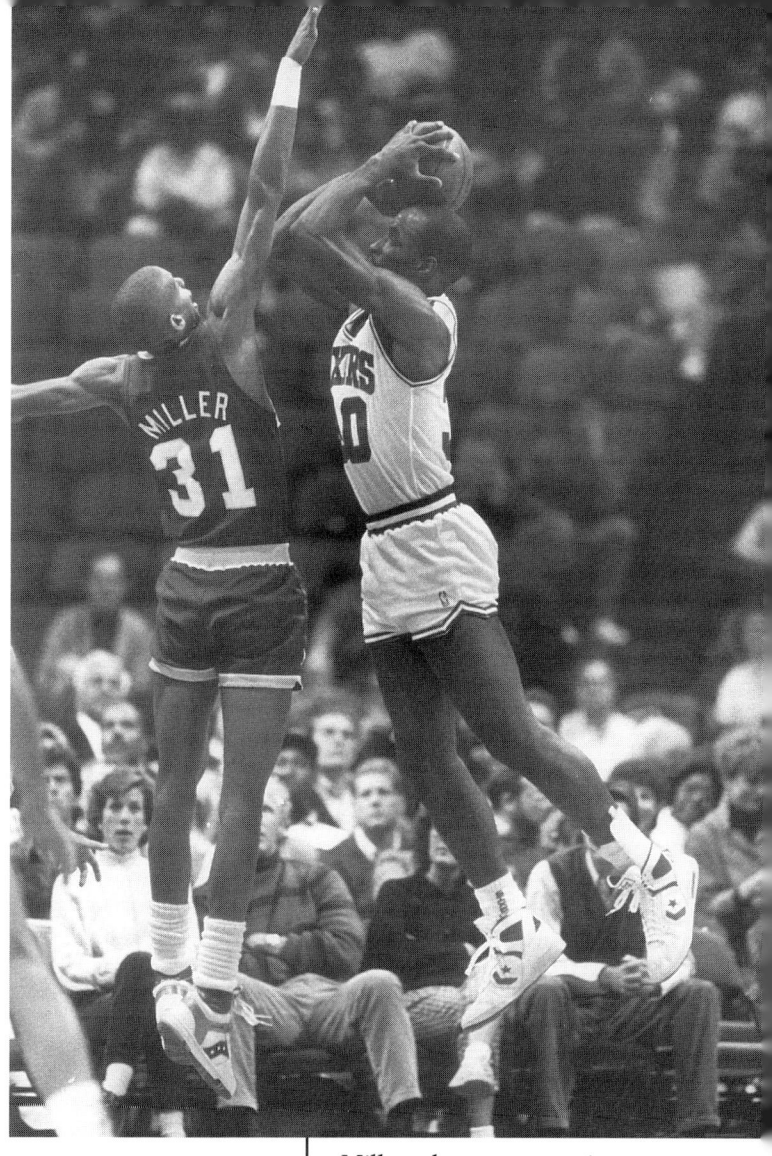

Miller plays aggressive defense, as Vincent Askew of the Philadelphia 76ers discovers.

REGGIE MILLER

posedly a better all-around player than Miller, Hopson lasted just a few seasons in the NBA. The Clippers ignored Miller to take another 6'7" Reggie, forward Reggie Williams of Georgetown. The team cited Williams's leadership skills as well as a history of performing in big games.

Reggie takes a jump-shot over Olden Polynice of the Clippers.

Williams has been little more than a journeyman in the NBA.

Of course, not all other choices were poor ones. Guards Kenny Smith and Kevin Johnson were picked ahead of Miller; both point guards became solid pros. An unknown forward from an unknown college—the University of Central Arkansas—went with the fifth pick. The Chicago Bulls have had no regrets in giving up Olden Polynice to the Seattle SuperSonics in order to move up in the draft and nab Scottie Pippen.

The Pacers had the 11th choice — and a dilemma. The year before, the Pacers were heavily criticized by fans and media when they selected Chuck Person, a forward from Auburn, instead of Michigan State's Scott Skiles, the most valuable player of the Big Ten and a local hero. Fans who had come to Market Square Arena to watch the 1986 draft booed loudly.

Once again in 1987, the Pacers invited the faithful to the arena. And when general manager Donnie Walsh stood at the podium, his team's fans desperately wanted him to choose Indiana University hero Steve Alford, a first-team All-America guard.

When Walsh announced that the Pacers were choosing Reggie Miller, boos cascaded from all around Market Square Arena.

Walsh was not surprised by the reaction. "This is Indiana," he said with a hint of a smile. "Taking Person last year over Skiles was worse. Alford's a bigger situation, because he was a bigger name, very popular around here."

Miller did not expect to have his selection booed. But he didn't back away from it, either. "I play off the crowd," he said. "That's what takes care of me, the yelling and the excitement and the whoop-de-do. That's my high, a sensation I can't describe. Indiana is a basketball state. They know the game, they know the players, they understand basketball."

Perhaps, but the fans who felt disappointed and betrayed had not done their research. They had seen Alford lead his college to the national title three months before and they were hoping his success would transfer over to the Pacers. Miller, on the other hand, had never gotten UCLA into the Final Four.

Walsh was not worried about the immediate reaction. He knew—and most basketball insiders knew—that Alford was too short and too slow to make it in the NBA. (Alford did get picked in the second round of the draft but his pro career was very short.)

If fans had read the tipsheets, they would have gathered that there were knocks against Reggie. Supposedly, he was unwilling to give up the ball, no matter what. He may have been "unrefined" and not real coachable.

"What makes me a selfish player?" Miller wondered. "Because I shoot the ball? I'm supposed to shoot the ball. That's how you score points. Those points go on the scoreboard for the whole team."

One person understood the dynamics of draft-day receptions—Chuck Person. He had heard the boos, but he didn't let them bother him. He was able to win the fans over quickly with his sharp shooting and aggressive style of play. In the previous year, he made Walsh look like a smart man when he earned the NBA's Rookie of the Year honors.

"The fans know that Donnie is a good general manager, and he's going to make the right decisions," Person said. "I thought it was hilarious that they booed me. Once they got to see me play, all that changed. It will probably be the same thing for Reggie. All they need is to see him play."

In 1987, the Pacers were coached by Jack Ramsay, who in 1991 would be inducted into the Basketball Hall of Fame. It was Ramsay, more than anyone, who sought to draft Miller. And it was Ramsay who told Miller to keep on shooting and to take advantage of the three-point shot.

So, in his first season, Reggie broke Larry Bird's rookie record for three-pointers. Bird, of course, is even more of a legend in Indiana than, well, Steve Alford.

That record fell on the next-to-last weekend of the season. Reggie was well aware of it as he approached the mark of 58. "I've known about the record for some time and have been pressing for it since I got the 57th [four games ago]," said Miller. "It's tough enough when you're going after those kinds of things, but when it's a record set by Larry Bird, well, that makes it really special for me and for the fans here."

Miller established the record with 16 seconds left in the first half of a victory over the Philadelphia 76ers. The first person to congratulate him on the sidelines was Ramsay, who had shown such faith in the youngster.

In Reggie's rookie year, Miller played in every game, averaging 22 minutes and 10 points. By the end of the season, it was clear the Pacers soon would be building around Miller.

"There are a lot of adjustments you have to make in that first year, and I went through them just like any other rookie," Reggie said. "There was the longer schedule; the NBA season is three times as long as the college season. You have to learn to pace yourself, get the right amount of rest between games and stay mentally sharp as well as ready physically."

Miller had to get used to many other things as well. "There also was the adjustment to living away from home. I'm real close with my family and I'd never been so far away from them. And it was tough adjusting to living in a place that you don't know very well and have to get used to. And there's also having to learn to be a professional. It becomes your job, your way of making a living, and the expectations really rise. Not just your expectations, but everyone's."

One teammate and friend who helped Miller adjust was John Long. "When I first got here, John was the two guard. If anybody taught me how to defend and how to play the two guard, it was John. John was a great shooter and defender and he knew all the other guards in the league. There would be nights before some games, he'd tell me to watch for something a guy does. I'd be sitting on the bench early on, and sure enough, somebody would do exactly what John said they would do. So when I got into the game, I would know what to look for."

Chuck Person helped Reggie too. Person is one of the NBA's prime trash-talkers. In a classic 1991 playoff series against Boston, it was Person who forced the Celtics to the limit, boasting he would be unstoppable, then backing it up on the court. "Chuck taught me how hard-nosed you have to be in the NBA. He's a true competitor," Miller added with a smile, "and he talks a lot."

As a rookie, Miller held back on the verbal stuff. He hadn't done enough on the court—he didn't even make the All-Rookie squad. And he understood that you have to walk the walk before you can talk the talk.

In the NBA, Reggie was just learning to crawl.

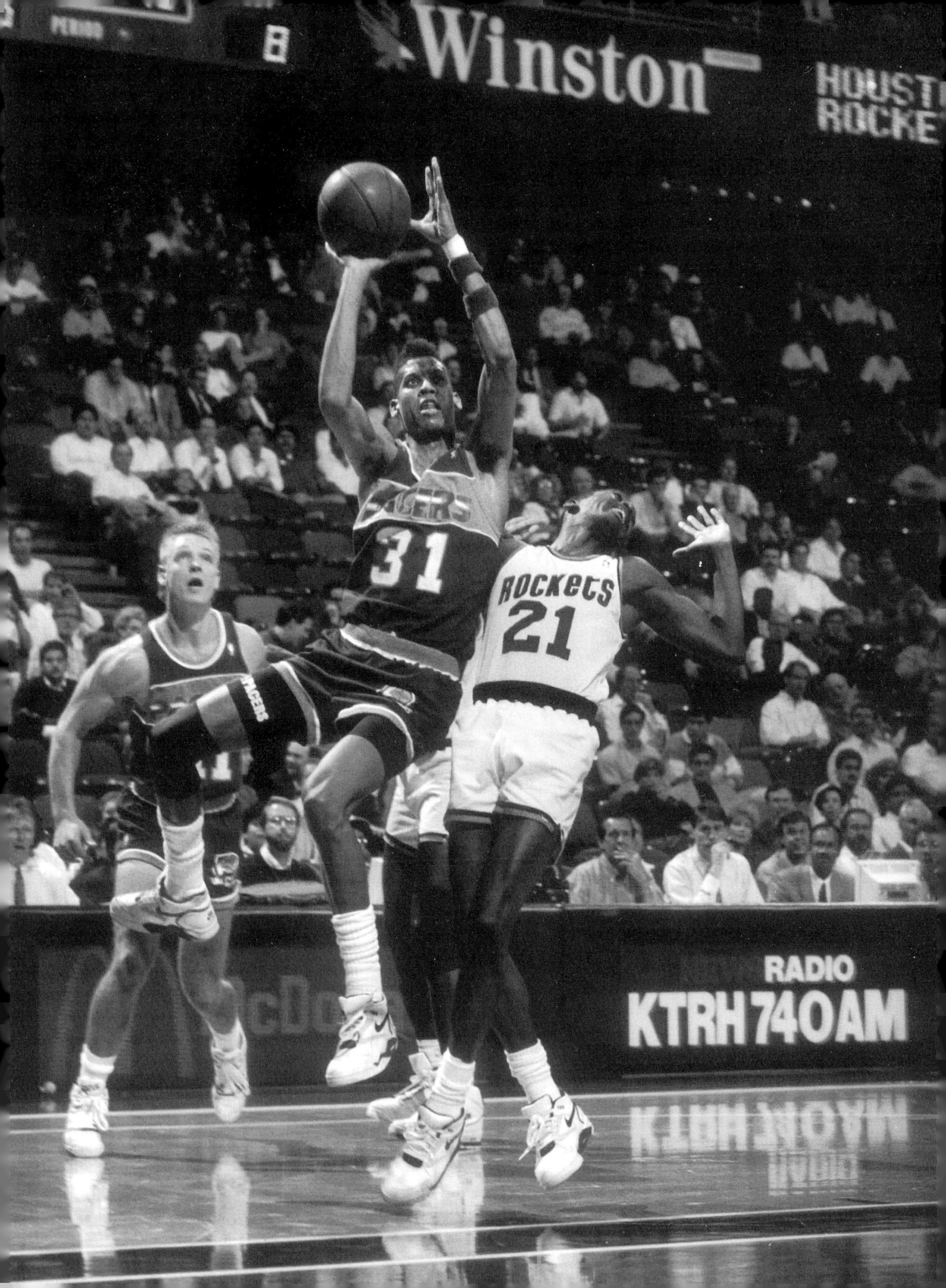

Winston
HOUST
ROCKE
31
ROCKETS
21
PACERS
RADIO
KTRH 740 AM

5
ALL-STAR

Reggie had often shown flashes of greatness as a rookie and had posted a respectable average of 10 points per game. But in order to be more than a role player, he had to expand his skills.

"In this league, you've always got to grow as a player. I think I began to grow up as a professional basketball player probably at the end of my second year, the last 30 or so games," said Miller. And indeed, Miller's average jumped from 16 points a game in that season.

Even though the Pacers finished 10 games worse in the standings than in his rookie year, Reggie showed progress.

"In this league, you've always got to grow as a player," said Miller. "You look at the Magic Johnsons and Michael Jordans and Larry Birds and they improve on something every year."

After his rookie season, Reggie knew his team wanted him to shoot the ball more. Here he obliges, knocking Houston Rocket guard Sleepy Floyd out of the way in order to put up a shot.

Jordan already had taught Miller a lesson. In an exhibition game, Reggie got carried away after holding Jordan in check for three periods, mouthing off about the achievement to His Airness. So Michael torched the Pacers for 20 points in the fourth quarter.

"We were walking off the court and Michael looked at me and said, 'Don't ever talk mess with me again,' and walked away," Miller recalled. "I was like, 'You're absolutely right, MISTER JORDAN.'"

Other lessons came less expensively as Miller, ever willing to learn, just kept on working. "I felt the best way to help myself was to get defenders off me by taking the ball to the hoop. My first couple of steps are quick, so why not drive? All summer after that season, I worked on driving, driving, driving, because everyone knows I can shoot."

Unfortunately, he was one of three Pacers who nearly always wanted to shoot. The other two were Detlef Schrempf and Chuck Person, whose nickname is "The Rifleman." That sometimes made for an uncomfortable situation. Miller felt he had to yield the scoring leadership to Person and sometimes he passed up good opportunities to shoot.

Coach Dick Versace spoke to the three players about it and, according to point guard Vern Fleming—whose job it is to spread the ball and the shots around—the Pacers listened. "Before, we went to Chuck too much and when that's all you do, it doesn't work," Fleming said. "Guys weren't getting along and were upset all the time. You can't win that way."

Person adapted, particularly in regard to Reggie. "We've spread the offense out and we're running more, and everyone's happy with the way the roles are set out," Person said. "I'm not the only focus of the offense any more, because Reggie has become such a big part of it and such a tough guy to stop, so there's no way I can be unhappy."

It would be Miller who was most thrilled, making the All-Star game in his third season, an eventful campaign in which the Pacers would become a playoff team.

Early in the schedule, while Indiana was keeping pace with the NBA's best, Miller was involved in a near-brawl against the Atlanta Hawks. In fact, he thought he should have been ejected for fighting in the first half of what turned into a 105-98 victory.

Miller had been in a running verbal battle with Atlanta's John Battle. Battle's teammate Doc Rivers jumped to his defense—by trying to choke Miller.

Rivers had a choke hold on Miller when he was ejected. Either the refs forgave or missed Miller's initiating the battle. "I was surprised that I wasn't thrown out," Miller said after a second-quarter incident.

Miller had some terrific matchups against Michael Jordan, but Jordan's Bulls were always a bit too strong for the Indiana Pacers. Here Jordan soars as Reggie is too late for the block and Mark Jackson hopes to draw a charging foul.

While Reggie's overall game was changing, his verbal assaults remained the same. "I love being the villain," he said. "You've got to remember the NBA is entertainment, like Billy Joel or Michael Jackson putting on a show is entertainment. When we take the floor, we have to perform, entertain people. You want to put on your best possible show. That's part of the ticket, I guess.

"And I love being booed. The bad guys are supposed to wear black. That's OK. I'll be the bad guy."

But Reggie could be the good guy too. In a victory over Chicago, Miller outscored Jordan 44-35. Reggie hit 13 of 22 shots, including four three-pointers, with Jordan guarding him.

"I love playing Michael. This is something to tell my kids," said Miller. "If you can't get psyched up to play Chicago and Michael Jordan, you do not need to lace up."

Miller also made an off-hand comment that the Bulls weren't much without Jordan, which later would haunt Miller and the Pacers. Chicago won four titles in six seasons, while Indiana didn't even get to the finals once.

Miller got to the All-Star Game for the first time in the 1989-90 season. Selected to the East All-Star team for the first time, Reggie also took part in the long-distance bombing of the three-point contest the night before the game. He lost by one point to Craig Hodges of Chicago, but did better than Jordan and Larry Bird.

Reggie played only 14 minutes and scored just four points in the All-Star Game. That mattered little to him.

"To step on the court and be surrounded by Larry Bird and Charles Barkley and Patrick Ewing and Isiah Thomas and Michael Jordan on my team, and then to see Magic Johnson and Karl Malone and Hakeem Olajuwon and John Stockton on the other side, that's really something," he said. "I'd say that's pretty good company."

Miller completed 1989-90 with a 24.6 scoring average, tops on the Pacers and eighth in the league. He made 150 three-point shots.

By now, Reggie had adjusted to life in Indiana, too. He had his own television show on local cable, and did a weekly radio report for an FM station. "We discuss anything the audience is interested in, and it definitely does not have to be about basketball," Reggie said. "If there is someone who wants to get something off their chest, or just talk about issues that are important to them, we do it. And if they just want to talk ball, well, we do that, too."

Miller became involved with several charities, most notably the United Negro College Fund and the Cystic Fibrosis Foundation. "Magic Johnson got me hooked on that," Miller said of the UNCF. "After my first year, he invited me to his 'Midsummer Night's Magic' [an exhibition all-star game benefitting the fund]. At the banquet, you see all these kids there and you see the joy that is in their eyes that they have to opportunity to go to school, to maybe become the next doctor or cure cancer or AIDS, or become the next lawyer or, who knows, the next president. It kind of sends a tingle down your spine. Anything I can do to help out, I'm going to do."

As for being a Midwesterner, well, even that was getting comfortable for the guy who once dubbed himself "Hollywood." "I love it here, because the people are so nice," he said. "When I first came here, of course, I didn't like it, because it took me out of California and I was singing the blues because of the weather. But the next few years were great. There's no traffic, no pollution, and it's very laid-back and comfortable. In L.A. people are always worried about what they look like. It's very materialistic there, but here, it's just simple, and I like it like that."

He also liked what he was seeing at Market Square Arena. The Pacers were becoming a contender—they have made the playoffs in every season since Reggie's third year—and the stands were filling up. "I was around when there were 4,000 or 5,000 people going to our games. You help build the program and now you are selling out games," he said. "People are wearing Pacers paraphernalia—you have a sense of pride in helping create that."

Miller was creating a stir with his on-court work. He averaged more than 20 points a game for the 1990-91, 1991-92, and 1992-93 seasons. He became one of the most dangerous long-range shooters in the NBA. Opponents prepared to stop Miller first, then worried about the other Pacers.

The organization fully realized it needed to build around Reggie, so Person was traded in September 1992. Schrempf was dealt away a little more than a year later. Indiana concentrated on bringing in strong rebounders and defenders, leaving much of the scoring to Miller.

Miller responded. On November 28, 1992, at Charlotte, he had one of those nights everyone in the building wouldn't forget—least of all Kendall Gill, who held Miller to 15 points in their previous meeting.

This time, Gill was forced to watch from the bench with a sprained ankle while Miller was guarded—sort of—by Dell Curry, David Wingate, Kevin Lynch, and even forward Larry Johnson. None could do much as Reggie went for a Pacers' record 57 points. "They didn't have anyone who could guard him," Schrempf said. "So we just kept calling his number."

Miller, who scored 45 points in the middle two periods, made 16 of 29 shots, including four three-pointers. He was 21 of 23 from the free-throw line in the best performance in the NBA.

The big outing followed a two-hour team meeting in which one subject was Miller Time—or the lack of it. Coaches and teammates told Reggie he needed to be even more aggressive with the ball and to put it up more.

"I wasn't being Reggie, and enough was enough," Miller admitted. "I'm ready to reclaim my title and that is being the second-best shooting guard in the East."

By now, number 31 was the most popular jersey in Indiana. Miller already had become number one with Pacers fans. "Kids ring the doorbell the entire summer," said his wife, Marita, whom Reggie married in 1992. "It used to be two a day, but now it's 25. They used to knock at the front door, but now, if we don't answer it, they come around to the back."

Miller carried his wife Marita on the court after the Pacers defeated the Atlanta Hawks in the 1994 playoffs.

Miller torched the Knicks for eight points in the last 18 seconds as he singlehandedly stole a game for the Pacers in the 1995 playoffs. Greg Anthony of the Knicks tried to defend.

A successful model who has appeared in commercials for everything from McDonald's to Maybelline, Marita also is an actress. She and Reggie are considered one of Indianapolis's most striking couples, even though they often can be found at home, lounging around and avoiding the spotlight.

Of course, when he gets onto the basketball court, Miller always seems to find the spotlight.

By 1994, when he had his greatest game in the playoffs at New York, special things were expected from Reggie.

As if any Knicks fan would forget what Miller did to their team in what some refer to as the "Spike Lee Game," Miller had even more pain in store for New York rooters in 1995.

In the opening playoff game in the Eastern Conference semifinals, back at the Garden, Miller once more staged the kind of late heroics that can ruin your day if you're rooting for the home team, as more than 19,000 people were. The Knicks led 105-99 with 18 seconds remaining. Sewed up, right?

"Realistically," said Pacers coach Larry Brown, "I thought we had no chance."

So Reggie got unreal. Off an inbounds play, Miller fired in a three-pointer. He'd missed 11 of 16 shots thus far, and with each miss the crowd would howl in delight. But he nailed this one.

Then, with the Knicks struggling to get the ball in, Miller made a steal. Replays showed he fouled John Starks to get to Anthony Mason's pass, but no referee blew his whistle. Smartly, Miller dribbled back two steps to the three-point line and hit another.

"You have to stick the dagger in," he said.

In three seconds, Miller had turned a lost situation into a tie game.

Loud boos from the crowd accompanied big smiles from Reggie and lots of chest-thumping.

"People pay big money to see a game, so why not have some fun with them? They say something to you, you say something back. It's still a game," he said.

"There are so many people out there working 9 to 5. The boss gets on them, the wife is screaming at them for not being affectionate enough, for not bringing flowers. So they come here to get away from all that. Then that's my job, to give them a show and make them forget for two hours. Let them take their frustrations out on me."

The Knicks successfully threw an inbounds pass, but they still seemed ready to fold as long as Reggie stayed revved up.

John Starks missed two free throws. Patrick Ewing grabbed the rebound, but failed on a short shot.

The ball came to—who else?—Miller, and he was fouled by Mason.

The fans were in a frenzy. Reggie was loving it. "Like they say, 'New York, New York. If you can make it there, you can make it anywhere.'"

Reggie made two foul shots and Indiana had stolen Game 1 of a series it would win in seven.

"All great players rise to the occasion," Miller said. "You look at Michael and Magic and those types of great players, they've had those moments people associate them with.

"Michael's a perfect example," he continued. "When he hit that shot against Cleveland to win a playoff series [in 1989], that's where it started for him, where he became bigger than basketball. That was the first stamp, even though he scored 63 points in a playoff against Boston. That was the shot that really catapulted him to stardom."

After sinking the Knicks, the Pacers got to face the Orlando Magic for the right to go to the NBA Finals. The two teams almost had as much history between them as the Pacers and Knicks—for two years straight, Indiana had caused the Magic's season to end early. In 1993, the two teams had identical records of 41-41, but because the Pacers had won the head-to-head series, they got to go to the playoffs while Orlando stayed home. In 1994, the Magic made their first playoffs, but Indiana made them feel unwelcome, sweeping them in the first round.

In 1995, however, the Magic, paced by Shaquille O'Neal and Penny Hardaway, was not going to be a pushover. In the conference finals, the two teams fought a hard-fought seven-game series. Orlando prevailed and won the right to play the Houston Rockets for the NBA championship.

Still, Reggie had clearly brought his game to a new level. And he was now a certifiable legend.

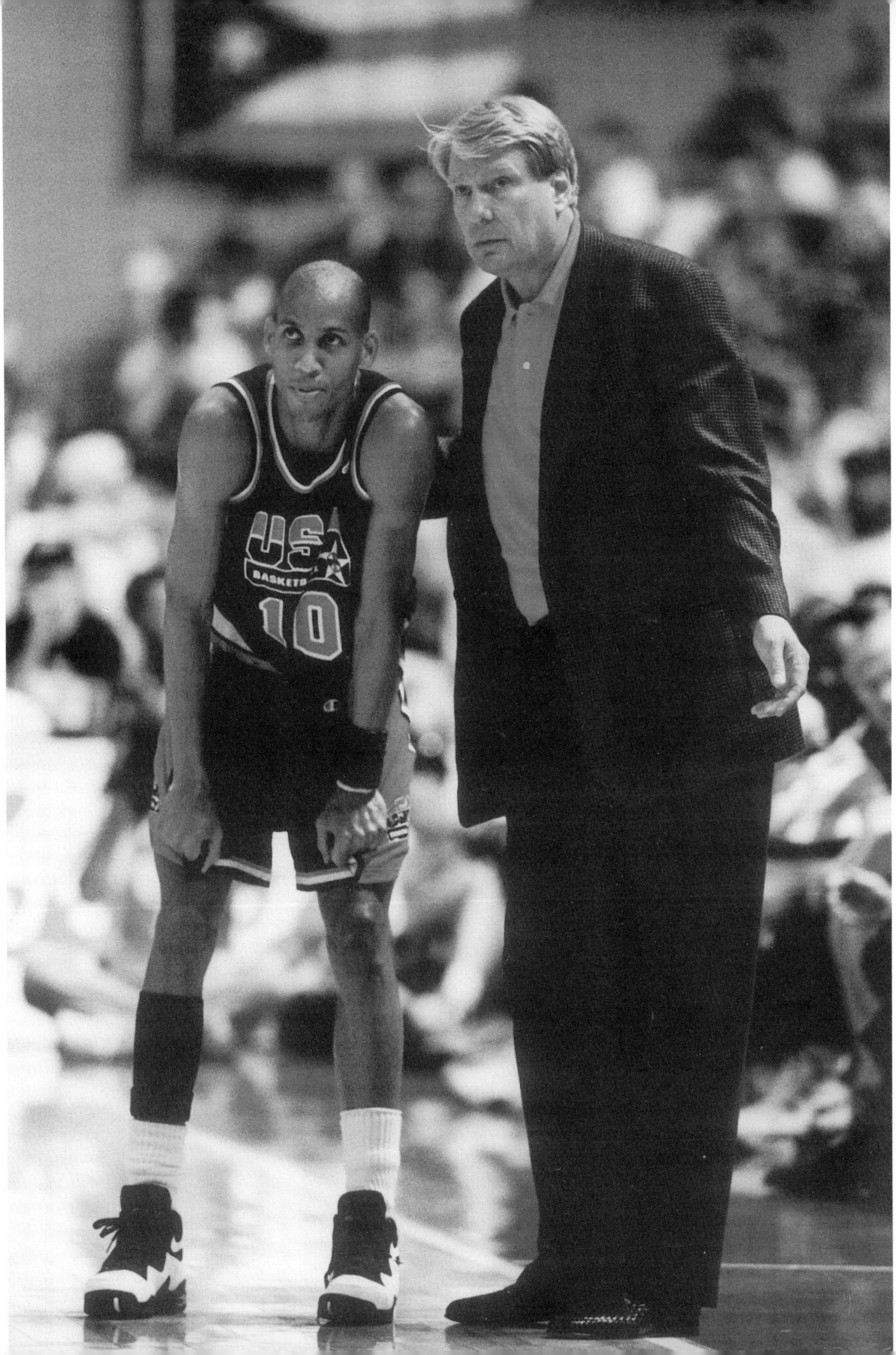
USA
10

6
DREAM-TEAMER

For decades, the United States sent college players into international competition. At the Olympics and the World Championships, they would rout all comers, winning gold medal after gold medal. Then, in 1972, the American team, in perhaps the most controversial—and certainly the worst-officiated—basketball game in Olympic history, were beaten by a point by the Soviet Union.

Most people felt it was a blip on the basketball screen, a fluke. So college players continued to represent America against foreign teams manned by professionals, players who stayed together most of the year, practicing and playing as a unit. But in the late 1980s, the United States hit a bigtime slump. The college kids, despite being All-Americans at home, couldn't match up with the older, more polished and experienced professionals representing the Soviet

Head coach Don Nelson talks with Miller during one of Dream Team II's early games.

Union and Yugoslavia. Even teams from Spain and Italy were suddenly giving the U.S. teams a run for their money.

"We were sending boys to play against men," Reggie Miller said. "We were sending teams that got together for a month to play teams that played together for years."

When the international basketball federation decided to allow anyone to play in the Olympics and World Championships, the NBA agreed to send its best. And the Dream Team was born. Miller's star was rising rapidly in 1992, but he wasn't nearly at the level where he was considered to join Michael Jordan, Magic Johnson, Larry Bird, Karl Malone and the rest of what some have called the greatest team ever assembled. He didn't mind—he knew his time would come.

In 1994, it did. Miller, coming off a strong season and a spectacular playoffs, was a key member of Dream Team II, which represented the United States at the World Championships in Toronto, Canada.

"It's almost been like a fairy tale ride," he said. "We always knew we [the Pacers] could go far. It was just a matter of going out to do it. And on top of that, being named to the Dream Team; there's no better feeling than knowing you're one of the 12 or 13 guys your country picks to represent it."

Also on the team were Derrick Coleman, Joe Dumars, Tim Hardaway, Larry Johnson, Alonzo Mourning, Shawn Kemp, Dan Majerle, Shaquille O'Neal, Mark Price, Steve Smith, Kevin Johnson, and Dominique Wilkins. While Dumars, Wilkins, and Price were relative old-timers, the majority of the team was made up of the young guns of the NBA. They were brash, talked trash, and made lots of cash.

While not the equal of the first Dream Team, Reggie knew this club could be just as dominant. "I don't want everyone to think that this is just fun," Miller said as the team practiced before heading to Canada. "This is very serious for me.

"After the success of Dream Team I, a lot of expectations are going to be put on us," he continued. "I want to have the same accomplishments as Dream Team I. I don't want to call a timeout throughout the whole competition. I want to beat teams by 30, 40, 50 points. I want to show the rest of the world that basketball is king in America. I want to destroy the competition. I don't even want it to be close. I want it to be a laugher."

It was. The Americans romped through the world and the World Championships like it was just another outing against an expansion team. But unlike the first Dream Team, which except for Charles Barkley's shoving match with an Angolan player conducted itself with class on and off the court, this one drew attention for its behavior. Too much showboating, the critics said. Too much anger. Except for the veterans, this group was too loud, too boastful, and immature.

Miller was part of that, of course. Remember, this is a guy who once got Michael Jordan so mad that he head-butted and took a swing at Miller, an incident Jordan says he regrets as much as any in his unequaled career.

Through it all, Miller was playing great basketball. Against Puerto Rico, he was unstoppable, hitting eight three-pointers and scoring 26 of his 28 points in the first half, personally outscoring the Puerto Ricans in a 62-25 half.

Amazingly, this was the second time in a row he had managed that feat. In the previous game against Australia, he knocked down five three-pointers and outscored the opposition 51-49 by himself.

"I might have had a Spike Lee flashback," Miller said.

At one point, Reggie put in 21 of 35 treys. Naturally, it helped that in international play, the three-point line is 20 feet, 7 inches away from the basket, well inside the NBA line.

"You can't put this three-point distance in the NBA," Miller said. "These are shots centers can hit. I like it just the way it is for the NBA. The NBA distance separates the men from the boys."

Miller also helped the United States get revenge against Russia, which won the 1988 Olympics (when it was known as the Soviet Union). Just weeks before, the Russians had beaten a U.S. college team at the Goodwill Games, and Reggie didn't like that.

"That's one game that was marked on our schedules before this began," Miller admitted. "We saw how they pushed around our young boys over there in Russia. We're sending in their big brothers. Let's see if they do all that pushing now."

Of course, they couldn't. In the championship game, the Americans won by 46 points. When the world title was won, Reggie and several teammates claimed Dream Team II was as good as the first Dream Team. To which Jordan responded, "Those guys are on the right team, because they're definitely dreaming."

Reggie still was dreaming about something else: the 1996 Olympics. He wanted to be in Atlanta, part of Dream Team III, and get a shot to equal the gold medal his sister Cheryl won in 1984.

"Winning the World Championships was a great experience, but it isn't the Olympics, which is the number one thing outside of the NBA," he said. "Being on that team in Atlanta is important to me, and I think I've earned being considered."

Coach Lenny Wilkens called him an automatic choice. "Reggie has proven himself and that he belongs with this great group of players," Wilkens said when Dream Team III was chosen.

Miller certainly liked what he saw on the roster. There were Malone, John Stockton, Scottie Pippen, Charles Barkley, and David Robinson, who had all played on the 1992 squad. And there were Anfernee Hardaway, Grant Hill, Hakeem Olajuwon, Shaquille O'Neal, Mitch Richmond, and Gary Payton as well.

"This team is really deep, more so even than Dream Team II," Miller said. "We are really strong in the center position, with Hakeem, David, and Shaq. We have two of the greatest point guards in Penny [Hardaway] and Stockton, and we have the most talented small forward in the game today in Scottie Pippen."

But he wasn't as impressed with the squad as O'Neal was.

Federico Lopez of Puerto Rico (left) offers little defense as Miller pops another three pointer. Miller scored 26 points in the first half of the 1994 game.

"This Dream Team could take on all the other Dream Teams put together," Shaq said.

Not quite. That was proved throughout the Olympics, when this U.S. squad actually struggled in several games. Rarely were things decided by halftime, as they were in Barcelona.

Some of the Americans were playing selfishly, not passing the ball or putting up one bad shot after another. Others showboated too much, trying to make no-look passes or to slam-dunk the ball from the free-throw line. Reggie, however, often lent a calming influence when on the court, playing textbook basketball. Of course, he knocked down a number of three-pointers that staggered opponents' comebacks. In the end, no other team could match the depth of Dream Team III—or their defense.

Miller hardly minded that he didn't particularly stand out during the Games. He stood high when the gold medals were presented, and nobody was smiling more broadly.

"Hey, Cheryl, look what I've got," he shouted, holding up his gold medal. "Now we've both got one."

Dream Team members listen to the national anthem during medal ceremonies for men's basketball at the 1996 Olympics. From left to right are: David Robinson, Scottie Pippen, Mitch Richmond, Reggie Miller, Karl Malone, and Shaquille O'Neal.

STATISTICS

REGGIE MILLER

Regular Season

SEASON	G	FGM	FGA	Pct	FTM	FTA	Pct	3PM	3PA	Pct	RBD	AST	PTS	AVG
1987-88	82	306	627	.488	149	186	.801	61	172	.355	190	132	822	10.0
1988-89	74	398	831	.479	287	340	.844	98	244	.402	282	227	1181	16.0
1989-90	82	664	1287	.514	544	627	.868	150	362	.414	295	311	2016	24.6
1990-91	82	596	1164	.512	551	600	.918	112	322	.348	281	331	1865	22.6
1991-92	82	562	1121	.501	442	515	.858	129	341	.378	318	314	1695	20.7
1992-93	82	571	1193	.479	427	485	.880	167	399	.427	258	262	1736	21.2
1993-94	79	524	1042	.503	403	444	.908	123	282	.421	212	248	1574	19.9
1994-95	82	505	1092	.482	383	427	.897	195	470	.415	210	242	1586	19.6
1995-96	76	504	1066	.473	430	498	.863	136	410	.410	214	253	1606	21.1
1996-97	81	552	1246	.443	418	475	.880	229	536	.427	286	273	1751	21.6
Totals	801	5179	10,669	.485	4033	4597	.877	1432	3568	.401	2556	2593	15824	19.8

Playoffs

SEASON	G	FGM	FGA	Pct	FTM	FTA	Pct	3PM	3PA	Pct	RBD	AST	PTS	AVG
1989-90	3	20	35	.571	19	21	.905	3	7	.429	12	6	62	20.7
1990-91	5	34	70	.488	32	37	.865	8	19	.421	16	14	106	21.6
1991-92	3	25	43	.581	24	30	.800	7	11	.538	7	14	81	27.0
1992-93	4	40	75	.533	36	38	.942	10	19	.526	12	19	126	31.5
1993-94	16	121	270	.448	94	112	.839	35	83	.422	48	48	371	23.2
1994-95	17	138	200	.478	104	121	.868	54	128	.422	51	38	434	25.5
1995-96	1	7	12	.412	13	15	.867	2	6	.333	1	1	29	29.0
Totals	49	385	800	.481	322	374	.861	119	273	.436	157	128	1211	24.7

G	games	FTM	free throws made	RBD rebounds
FGM	field goals made	FTA	free throws attempted	AST assists
FGA	field goals attempted	3PM	three-point shots made	PTS points
Pct	percent	3PA	three-point shots attempted	AVG average

REGINAL WAYNE MILLER A CHRONOLOGY

1965 Born August 24 in Riverside, California

1983 Decides to enter UCLA, crosstown rival of USC—his sister Cheryl's college

1985 Leads UCLA to NIT championship; is named MVP of the tournament

1986 Sets UCLA record by successfully shooting 202 free throws in one season

1987 Leads Bruins to a 25-7 record and a Pacific-10 Conference title; is drafted by Indiana Pacers

1990 Is named to All-Star Game for first time

1994 In perhaps the greatest shootout in playoff history, Reggie scores 25 points in the final quarter of Game 1 to sink the New York Knicks; helps U.S. to a gold medal at the World Championships

1995 In another playoff game against the Knicks, Reggie scores six points in two seconds to turn around a lost game; Reggie is named to the All-Star Game for second time

1996 Again named to the All-Star Team; helps steady Dream Team III on their way to a gold medal at the Olympics

SUGGESTIONS FOR FURTHER READING

Callahan, Gerry, "Floored!" *Sports Illustrated,* May 15, 1995.

Lupica, Mike, "Mr. Big Shot." *Esquire,* December 1994.

MacMullan, Jackie, "Keeping Pacers." *Sports Illustrated,* May 20, 1996.

Miller, Reggie, with Gene Wojciechowski, *I Love Being the Enemy.* New York: Simon & Schuster, 1995.

Thorley, Stew, *Sports Great, Reggie Miller.* Springfield, NJ: Enslow Publishers, 1996.

ABOUT THE AUTHOR

Barry Wilner has been a sports writer for the *Associated Press* for 20 years. In that time, he has covered the Super Bowl, Olympics, World Cup, Stanley Cup finals, and many other major sporting events. He has written books on hockey, soccer, swimming, and Olympics sports, including *Dan Marino, Mark Messier, Superstars of Men's Golf,* and *Superstars of Women's Golf* for Chelsea House.

PHOTO CREDITS: AP Wide World Photos: 2, 10, 11, 18, 29, 32, 36, 42, 45, 50, 60; Reuters/Corbis-Bettmann: 8, 49, 54, 59; Courtesy UCLA Sports Information Department: 16, 24; National Baseball Library: 21; UPI/Bettmann: 26, 35.

INDEX

Abdul-Jabbar, Kareem, 25, 29
Ainge, Danny, 33
Alford, Steve, 37, 38
Anthony, Greg, 10, 13, 50
Austin, Alex, 26
Barkley, Charles, 46, 57, 59
Battle, John, 45
Bird, Larry, 33, 39, 46, 56
Brown, Larry, 14, 51
Carnesecca, Lou, 27
Chamberlain, Wilt, 21
Coleman, Derrick, 56
Curry, Dell, 49
Davis, Antonio, 14
Davis, Hubert, 10, 12, 13
Dumars, Joe, 56
Ewing, Patrick, 13, 46, 56
Farmer, Larry, 26
Fleming, Vern, 44
Floyd, Sleepy, 43
Gill, Kendall, 48
Gilliam, Armon, 35
Glass, Willie, 27
Goodrich, Gail, 25
Hardaway, Penny, 53, 59
Hardaway, Tim, 56
Harper, Derek, 12, 13
Hazzard, Walt, 25, 26, 27, 28, 31
Hill, Grant, 59
Hodges, Craig, 46
Hopson, Dennis, 35
Houston, Wade, 29
Jackson, Mark, 45

Johnson, Kevin, 27, 36, 56
Johnson, Larry, 49, 56
Johnson, Magic, 30, 47, 56
Johnson, Marques, 25
Jordan, Michael, 44, 45, 46, 47, 52, 56, 57, 58
Kemp, Shawn, 56
Lee, Spike, 11, 13, 14, 15
Letterman, David, 15
Long, John, 40
Lopez, Federico, 59
Lynch, Kevin, 49
Malone, Karl, 47, 56, 59, 60
Mason, Anthony, 51, 52
Miller, Carrie, 17, 18, 19
Miller, Cheryl, 17, 18, 19, 20–23, 25, 27, 28, 58, 60
Miller, Darrell, 17, 21
Miller, Marita, 13, 49–50
Miller, Reggie
  as a baseball player, 20
  honors received, 23, 29, 30–31
Miller, Saul, Jr., 17
Miller, Saul, Sr., 17, 18, 19, 20
Miller, Tammy, 17
Morrison, Stan, 35
Mourning, Alonzo, 56
Nelson, Don, 55
Olajuwon, Hakeem, 47, 59
Olson, Lute, 27
O'Neal, Shaquille, 53, 59, 60
Payton, Gary, 59

Parrish, Robert, 33
Person, Chuck, 37, 38, 39, 40, 44–45, 48
Pippen, Scottie, 36, 59, 60
Price, Mark, 56
Ramsey, Jack, 39
Richardson, Pooh, 29
Richmond, Mitch, 59, 60
Riley, Pat, 12
Rivers, Doc, 45
Robinson, David, 35, 59, 60
Schrempf, Detlef, 44, 48, 49
Scott, Byron, 30
Selvy, Furman, 21
Skiles, Scott, 37
Smith, Kenny, 36
Smith, Steve, 56
Starks, John, 9, 12, 13, 51, 52
Stockton, John, 47, 59
Thomas, Isiah, 47
Thompson, Bobby, 26
Tyson, Mike, 13
Versace, Dick, 44
Walsh, Donnie, 37–38
Walton, Bill, 25, 29
Wicks, Sidney, 25
Wilkens, Lenny, 59
Wilkins, Dominique, 56
Williams, Reggie, 35
Wingate, David, 49
Wooden, John, 23, 25